Christopher Davis's Best Year Yet

Lauren L. Wohl

Illustrated by Mike Reed

Hyperion Books for Children
New York

For Cliff,
for always
—L. L. W.

Printed in the United States of America.

FIRST EDITION
1 3 5 7 9 10 8 6 4 2

The artwork for each picture is prepared using pencil.
This book is set in 16 point Berkeley.

Library of Congress Cataloging-in-Publication Data

Wohl, Lauren L.
    Christopher / Lauren L. Wohl ; illustrated by Mike Reed. — 1st
ed.
      p.   cm.
    Summary: In the year that he becomes eight, Christopher gets his first pair of glasses, loses a tooth, gets a baby brother, takes piano lessons, and learns to play baseball.
    ISBN 0-7868-0106-9 (trade)—ISBN 0-7868-1083-1 (pbk.)
    [1. Family life—Fiction. 2. Baseball—Fiction. 3. Size—Fiction.]
I. Reed, Mike, ill. II.Title.
PZ7.W8176Ch   1995   94-26791
[E]—dc20

1
WINTER

The Flu Solution

Monday, January 29, was going to be the worst day of Christopher Davis's life ... unless he could figure out a way to avoid school. That's why on Thursday, January 25, Christopher was the first to volunteer to take Warren to the nurse's office.

It was in the middle of Math. Warren, the biggest boy in Mrs. Caputo's second grade, stood up without warning and announced, "I'm sick."

Every head turned toward the back of the room. Warren's skin had turned a color that was frankly a little scary.

Mrs. Caputo was immediately at his side. She put her hand to his forehead.

"My, my, Warren. You're quite warm. We've got to get you to the nurse."

She turned around to the class, and in that same second, Christopher raised his hand. He waved his hand. He lifted his body from his chair in anticipation.

"Perhaps Christopher can help you to her office," Mrs. Caputo suggested.

In a flash, Christopher was at Warren's seat. He put his arm around Warren's back and helped as best he could while Warren dragged himself up, then to the door, through the hall, and into the nurse's office.

The nurse took one look at Warren and told Christopher to return to the classroom and gather up Warren's books and personal belongings and bring them back.

At Warren's desk, Christopher touched everything. Warren's pencil—maybe he had chewed on it. Warren's notebook—maybe he had sneezed into it. An old sock—who knows what Warren had done with that? He took Warren's boots, coat, and scarf from the wardrobe, wrapped the scarf around his own neck, and delivered the whole bundle to the nurse.

"Warren's pretty sick, huh?"

"Looks like the flu," the nurse answered. "His mom is coming to pick him up."

"The flu, huh? Pretty serious. How long does it take?"

"Oh, Warren will probably be out for a week."

"No. I mean, how long does it take to catch it?" Christopher asked.

"I don't know. A couple of days, I guess."

The nurse looked at Christopher in a funny way. Before she could say anything more, Christopher turned to go.

"Bye, Warren," he called. "Feel better."

"Thanks, Chris," Warren whispered.

Thanks, Warren! is what Christopher thought.

On Friday morning, Christopher felt just fine. He guessed the flu would hit that afternoon, but Friday afternoon, Christopher felt even better. Saturday morning, however, he woke up with a stiff neck.

"Mom, my neck hurts."

"You must have slept wrong, Chris. It'll work itself out."

"Nope, I think it's the flu."

Christopher's mother put her lips to his forehead.

"Cool as a cucumber."

"A lot of kids in my class have the flu. It's contagious. Maybe I've caught it."

"I don't think so, dear. You had a shot in November. Dr. Levin wanted to be sure no one in the family got the flu this winter because of the baby."

His mother patted her belly.

"Oh," said Christopher.

That baby! is what Christopher thought.

The Tell-All Solution

On Sunday night, January 28, after dinner and after the seven o'clock weather update, Christopher asked his mother if they could talk.

"What's cooking?" she asked.

"Mom. I need a day off from school. I just feel like I've got to have some time to relax."

"Oh."

His mother's "oh" usually meant "go on," so Christopher did.

"Second grade is a lot harder than I thought. I'm not really doing so well."

Christopher paused, but his mother just waited. She looked worried.

"I know I had a good report card, but that was just on first-grade stuff."

"Is it something in particular that

you're finding difficult, Christopher?"

"It's everything." Christopher swallowed hard. "I can't read."

"What do you mean, Chris? You've been reading since last April."

"Only baby books. I can't read real books. The words are too hard."

"Have you talked to Mrs. Caputo? Would you like me to call her? She must know what's going on."

"I don't think so, Mommy. No one knows. And now it's too late. The reading test is tomorrow."

"Of course it's not too late, Chris. You just need to tell your teacher. "Tomorrow, first thing."

"Okay," Christopher said.

But what will I say? is what Christopher thought.

The Surprise Solution

When he got to room 201 on Monday morning, January 29, Mrs. Caputo wasn't there. A substitute teacher greeted the class.

"Good morning, children. I'm Mr. Hall. Please take your seats."

Christopher couldn't believe it. Mrs. Caputo was absent. The reading test would be canceled. Christopher's wish had come true. He hoped Mrs. Caputo wasn't too sick—he liked her and all—but he couldn't help smiling.

"As you know," the substitute teacher began, "Mrs. Caputo is going to be working with each of you individually today, in the reading laboratory. I'll be here, with the rest of you, as each one goes to see her."

What was this man saying? Christopher couldn't make sense of it. Mrs. Caputo wasn't absent after all? The reading test was on?

The Test

Mrs. Caputo called the children into the lab in alphabetical order. When Samantha Coburn returned to the classroom, she announced, in a most official way, "Christopher Davis is next."

Christopher found his way to the reading lab. Mrs. Caputo had her usual warm smile and a collection of books on her desk.

"Good morning, Christopher. Which of these appeals to you?"

Christopher pointed to a book with a bright yellow cover.

"Wonderful. Will you read it to me, please?"

Christopher opened the book to the title page. Slowly, deliberately, he read it to his teacher.

"Go on."

He turned to the first page of the story. He couldn't focus on the words. They were moving around. The black ink kept getting thicker and thicker and then it would just disappear as he tried to decipher a word.

"Christopher?"

Chris looked up. Mrs. Caputo knew he was crying, so there was no need to pretend.

"I can't read."

Mrs. Caputo looked confused.

"But you just read the title."

"That was easy. But I can't read this."

Mrs. Caputo turned back to the title page.

"Read it again," she told Christopher.

"The Big Day."

Now Mrs. Caputo turned to the first page of the story. "The first three words of the story are the same." She followed each one with her finger. "The big day . . ."

Now Christopher was confused.

"It's not the words, Chris. It's the size of the words. I think you need glasses."

"Glasses?"

"Yes. Have you ever had your eyes checked?"

"I don't think so."

"I'll call home this evening and talk to your parents about taking you to an ophthalmologist."

"Eye doctor."

"Yes, Christopher. An eye doctor."

Spectacles

On Thursday, February 1, after school, Christopher's mother took him to Dr. Mazer. The doctor asked Chris to read some letters from a wall chart. That part was easy. But when Dr. Mazer gave him a small card to read, Christopher couldn't make the letters out.

"Nothing to worry about. That's why you're here," the doctor assured Chris.

Then Dr. Mazer put the biggest, bulkiest, ugliest eyeglasses machine right on Christopher's nose, and he asked Christopher to read the letters on the card again.

"This is how I find out what lenses you need," Dr. Mazer explained.

The doctor kept changing the lenses in the machine. Each time, the letters got darker and bigger and clearer and easier for Christopher to see. At last they found exactly the right ones, and Christopher was fitted for a pair of eyeglasses.

"Spectacles, I like to call them," Dr. Mazer said.

A week later, Christopher got his spectacles. Dr. Mazer slipped them on Christopher's face and handed him a magazine. The words were small and close together, but they were clear.

"Read some of this to us," Dr. Mazer asked.

It was a regular grown-up's magazine. Didn't the doctor understand that he couldn't read? Christopher flipped through a few pages, looking at the pictures. He stopped at one of a base-

ball team dressed in ski gear, standing around a field. He started reading:

"With spring tra . . . training just weeks away, pl . . . players wonder if it will ever stop snowing. This has been a hard winter, with re . . . rec . . . cord snowfalls."

Christopher laughed out loud.

I'm reading, is what Christopher thought.

2

SPRING

Eight

Christopher's birthday arrived with the tulips. And every year, as soon as the weather showed the least sign of warming, he began measuring the days until his birthday by the flowers that bloomed in the garden. This year he started at the end of March.

Christopher rarely had to wear his heavy winter jacket anymore. The snow shovel was finally moved back down to the basement instead of standing at the ready in the front closet. The branches of the trees along the street seemed to be getting fatter, although they had no leaves yet. And the soil in

the flower beds had cracked; shoots of green were showing through—*if* you looked carefully enough for them.

In early April, the crocuses—first the white ones, then the purple—came up. Then the yellow daffodils, the pink hyacinths, and, finally, by the middle of the month, and just in time for Christopher's birthday party, the red tulips blossomed. It was *really* spring. And he was *really* eight!

The Tooth

Eight years old, so how could it be that Christopher had not lost one single baby tooth yet. Every other kid in his class, every other kid in the entire second grade, and probably every kid in the entire first grade already had.

Christopher asked his mother.

"People grow at different times, Chris. There's not a right time or a wrong time to lose baby teeth. There's just your time and someone else's time."

"*Everyone* else's time," Christopher corrected.

"Let's see."

Christopher plopped himself down on the couch and opened his mouth wide, wide, wider. His mother looked in.

"It's dark in there. And there's peanut butter and jelly leftovers in there. And yes, you're right, all your baby teeth are in there, too."

She put her pinkie on his two front teeth.

"Solid."

Then she put her pinkie on Christopher's lower teeth.

"What's this? Movement? Yes, I think so, Chris. This one is moving."

Christopher explored his bottom teeth with his tongue, pushing as hard as he could. He didn't feel any movement. He touched each tooth with his index finger. Solid. Solid. Oops. He tried again. Oops. Yup. Movement. He had a loose tooth. Well, maybe not an altogether loose tooth, but a loosening one. At last.

"Thanks, Mom."

It wasn't much, but Christopher had something to work on. In the weeks that followed, he chewed on every hard thing he could find: stale rolls, apples, licorice sticks, Gummi Bears, gummy snakes, gummy dinosaurs. And every day his tooth got a little bit looser. By the middle of May, he could jiggle it with the slightest touch of his tongue, and he did that every chance he got.

Soon his tooth was so loose he could twist it around with his fingers. But still it hung in there.

His father said the time had come, and he would gladly extract that tooth for Christopher. His brother offered to knock it out for Christopher. His mother said it would come out in its own good time.

And that's just how it happened. One

day, in school, when Christopher pushed his tooth with his tongue, the tooth simply let go and dropped out.

He raised his hand and asked if he could get a drink of water. Acting as if nothing all that special had just happened, he explained, "My tooth fell out, and it's bleeding."

Mrs. Caputo led him to the water fountain and wet a tissue for him.

"Put this on the space and apply a little pressure."

She handed Christopher another tissue and told him to wrap his tooth in it and take it home.

Christopher nodded.

The Tooth Fairy

As soon as he got home from school, Christopher unwrapped his treasure and examined it. The tooth was awfully small, and it had bits of dried blood at the bottom. He took it into the bathroom, filled a paper cup with warm water, and gave it a little bath and brushing. At dinner, he proudly showed it to his family.

"Guess you'll be having a visit tonight," his father said.

"Guess so."

Now Christopher had heard all sorts of theories from his friends about the tooth fairy. Zak was sure she existed. He'd even seen her. She wore a light blue silky gown that looked a little like a robe his mother had, and she half floated, half flew. When she lifted your head from your pillow so she could take your tooth and replace it with a dollar, you hardly felt anything, she was so gentle.

Megan said that the tooth fairy was evil and that she used the teeth she collected to put evil spells on people.

Warren said that parents were the tooth fairy. It was parents who came into your room and took your tooth and gave you a dollar.

Samantha agreed. In fact, she had proof. She'd found all her baby teeth in her mother's drawer.

"Now, if there were really a tooth fairy, how would my teeth have ended up in my mother's drawer?"

Christopher's brother would know the truth.

"Greg?"

"Hmmmm?"

"Did the tooth fairy bring you a dollar for every baby tooth you lost?"

"Nah."

"Greg, I'm sure the tooth fairy brought you money for your teeth," Dad said.

"Sure, she did, Dad. But I got fifty cents. I hear the price has gone up lately."

"That's what I hear, too," Dad agreed.

At bedtime, Christopher's parents gave him a special tuck-in. They checked three times under his pillow to be sure the tooth, neatly wrapped, was safe. They opened the shade just a little at the bottom so the tooth fairy could find her way into the house. They kissed Christopher on his forehead and wished him pleasant dreams.

Matthew

The next morning, Christopher forgot to check under his pillow because, from the very minute he woke up, he knew something was happening in the house.

He went to the kitchen, and there was his grandma, sitting at the table, reading the paper.

"Grandma?"

"Good morning, Chris. How are you this spectacular morning?"

"How come you're here, Grandma? Where's Mommy?"

"Your mom's at the hospital, Chris. Your baby brother was born last night. He and your mom are just fine. And your daddy is with them right now."

"We have a baby brother? What's he like?"

"His name is Matthew."

"Matthew."

"And we're going to find out what he's like soon. Your parents said you and Greg could stay home from school today so you can visit your mother and new brother at the hospital. How does that sound?"

"Terrific!"

Christopher went upstairs and looked at himself in the mirror. He was a big brother now—not the baby in the family. Did he look different? He smiled at this image, and he saw that space in his lower jaw. His missing tooth.

Christopher ran to his bed and lifted the pillow. There, still neatly wrapped, was his tooth. Untouched.

Greg was standing in the doorway to

his room.

"You know about our new brother, don't you?"

"Yup. Grandma told me."

"It happened in the middle of the night. Dad was running up and down the stairs, making about a million telephone calls, and packing up Mom's things. I'm surprised all the noise didn't wake you. There was so much confusion around here that even the tooth fairy got mixed up. She left this dollar under my pillow instead of yours."

Greg showed a dollar bill to Christopher.

"She did?"

"Looks that way to me, Chris. And you know the funniest part? She took one of my dirty tissues with her. She must have thought there was a tooth

wrapped up in it. Won't she be surprised?"

"She certainly will."

Christopher took the dollar from his brother.

"I'll leave my tooth under my pillow again tonight. Just in case the tooth fairy comes back looking for it."

"Good thinking, Chris."

And then Greg did a really funny thing. He hugged Christopher and kind of rocked him.

"Let's get dressed," Greg said. "We really ought to let Matthew meet his two big brothers. What do you say, Chris?"

"Absolutely!"

3

SUMMER

Three Years Ago

Christopher was five—just five—when his father told him for the first time:

"Baseball is your game."

That was the day his father gave him Greg's glove.

"But it's Greg's," Christopher protested.

"Greg wants you to have it," his father said. "He doesn't like baseball."

Christopher hesitated, and then, encouraged by his father's gestures, he slipped the glove on. His mother said the glove was too big, Christopher was too young, it was too soon. Besides, Greg might change his mind and want to give baseball another try.

But his father took Christopher to the park that afternoon anyway, and they played their first real game of catch—just the two of them.

And Chris *was* good right from the start. Grounders. Bouncers. Flies. It came easily: he'd put out his glove and, like magic, the ball ended up right in the pocket.

"Amazing," his father said. "A natural. Born for the game. Next spring, we'll put you in the peewee league.

Shortstop, I think. You know, I played shortstop."

Greg talked to him about it that evening.

"So, you like baseball, huh?" he began.

"I guess."

"Sounds like you've got a talent for it, too."

"Dad says."

"I hate it. And I'm just awful at it. The worst."

"I don't think you're bad at it, Greg."

But Greg wasn't listening.

"Everyone takes it so seriously. They forget it's just a game. I always feel like I'm letting everyone down: the coaches, the parents, my teammates, Dad—especially Dad! I'm always hoping that I won't have to play. But they have some stupid rule in Little League that says everyone gets to play in every game.

"They put me in at the end. Then, if we're winning, I'm the one who gets to make an error—like I did yesterday—and throw away the game."

"Maybe you'll change your mind, Greg. Yesterday was just a bad day. Mom says you might change your mind."

"Not about baseball."

"Dad gave me your glove."

"It's cursed."

Christopher got up and took the glove from the doorknob of the closet.

"You want it back?"

"No way. It's yours—if you can get it to work for you."

"Are you angry?"

"At you? Why would I be angry at you? It's not your fault that you're a natural."

"Greg . . ."

"Hmmmm?"

"What's a natural, anyway?"

"Go to sleep, Chris. You've got a busy summer ahead. Dad will have you practicing every day."

Greg was right. Christopher and his father worked on his catching and throwing all through that summer. But it didn't seem like work to Chris. For him, it *was* a game; it was fun. And getting better at it made him happy. Besides, he'd never spent so much time alone with his father before. And it was nice to be the center of his attention.

Two Years Ago

The next spring, Christopher joined the peewee league. There were no try-outs. You just went down to the field and signed up. There were no real teams, either. Every week, whoever showed up, played. They put you in the outfield or on first base or at short-stop—any position you hadn't tried before. It didn't much matter, because no one—not any one of them—could hit. Even when the pitcher—one of the coaches—aimed the baseball right at the bat, it was a rare kid who could connect.

Christopher was no exception. But it was clear that he was some kind of fielder. At the end of the season, coach Susan told Chris's father that Chris has a real talent for the game.

"Work on his hitting and you'll have a Hall of Famer there," she said, and she pulled off Chris's baseball cap and messed up his hair.

Over the next couple of months, well into autumn, that's just what they did. Chris and his dad, and sometimes Greg, would go to the ball field after dinner and work on his hitting. His father would pitch—nice, slow, easy—and he'd coach—"Keep the bat high; keep your eye on the ball; watch your timing; swing; swing now; follow through." Greg would squat behind Chris at the plate, catching and tossing the ball back to Dad.

"If you'd hit a few, Chris, I wouldn't be working so hard," he told his brother.

"I'm trying, Greg."

"I'm kidding, Chris."

Last Year

The next spring, Christopher joined Little League. He was put on a team, got a uniform and a position—shortstop. They had real practices and real games that the newspaper wrote about.

Christopher loved putting on his uniform, fresh from the dryer on the day of a game—the bright white, knee-length pants and the sparkling green-and-white shirt with his team's sponsor, "Bill and Joe's Deli," embroidered on the back, just above his number: 18.

He loved being in the field on warm, breezy days with the smell of newly cut grass all around him and the cheers of encouraging parents and excited kids filling the air. He enjoyed sitting in the dugout, waiting for his turn at bat, alongside his teammates, talking about the game so far and planning every move they'd make from that moment on. He liked the scary feeling of walking up to the plate, swinging the bat, taking his stance, and watching the pitcher throw the ball.

And in that moment when time just stopped, Christopher always believed that he was going to smash that ball. But he never did. And after a month, even though he was surely the best shortstop on any team, he began to play fewer and fewer innings.

Jeff, their batting coach, couldn't figure it out. How could a boy with an eye like Chris's, with timing like Chris's, be so bad at hitting? Then, at one practice, Jeff took his own cap off and put it on Chris's head.

"Try this. Maybe your cap's too small

and you're getting too much sun glare."

Chris stood at the plate and watched Jeff's slow and easy pitch come at him. He swung.

He heard it first: the cracking sound of the bat hitting the ball. He felt it second: a sting in his hand. He saw it third: the ball arching through the air, over the pitcher, out into center field. And then he heard Jeff's voice: "Run!"

Christopher tossed the bat down and headed for first base. He ran as hard as he could, staring only at the base. His foot touched the pad. Safe!

Jeff pulled the cap from Chris's head and tapped it on his knee.

"There you go. Easy enough? You've done it once. There's nothing stopping you from doing it again. Right?"

Jeff smiled and pulled his cap onto his own head.

"Looks like all you need is a bigger baseball cap, Chris."

"I kind of like yours, Jeff. Why don't we get a new cap for you, and I'll keep this one?"

Jeff didn't say anything.

"I think it's my lucky cap," Chris added.

"Superstitious already, Chris? You're really turning into a ballplayer now."

Jeff replaced the cap on Christopher's head and pulled it down over his ears.

"Maybe you can put some elastic in, to keep it on top of your head. It's yours."

"Thanks."

The next Sunday, Chris got a double. And in every game after that, he got at least one hit.

"It's the cap," Chris confided to Greg.

"Don't be silly. You're a natural."

This Year

When this season rolled around, Chris was assigned to a new team: Demi's Bakery. The uniform was red and white; the cap, bright red. Chris's lucky cap was green, and if he wore it with the new uniform, it was going to be obvious. He'd have a lot of explaining to do, and Chris wasn't up to that. He left it in his closet.

Demi's coaches weren't nearly as organized as Bill and Joe's had been, and in the first three practices, Chris never had a turn at bat. He'd take the field, and no one ever noticed that he stayed there all through practice. It wasn't until the first game of the season that Chris stood at the plate.

Three pitches. Three strikes.

"It happens," a teammate called. "You'll get 'em next time."

Next time, the pitcher threw a wild curve that hit Chris on the arm, and Chris took first. That loaded the bases, and the next batter, Mark Singer, hit a grand slam. As Chris ran home, coach Sandy gave him a high five and said, "Glad to have you on our team."

It didn't matter that Chris struck out for his next two at bats.

"Good game?" his mother asked when he got home.

"We won. Six to three."

"Good game?" she repeated.

"Okay."

During the next couple of games, Chris just couldn't get a hit. His coach asked him if everything was all right. Was Chris getting enough sleep? Didn't they have a new baby at home? Maybe that was throwing Chris off schedule.

"Maybe," Chris agreed.

But Chris knew that this had nothing to do with Matthew, with schedules, or with sleeping.

"You know, Chris," his mother said one afternoon, out of the blue, "if you've stopped enjoying baseball, you can stop playing."

"That's not it. I like it. I really do."

"Then . . . ?"

"I just can't get a hit without my lucky cap."

Chris explained about Jeff's baseball cap. He went upstairs and took the cap out of the closet.

"Let's see," his mother said, and she reached out for the cap.

"Jeff must have had this for lots of seasons of hard coaching. It's practically falling apart. But I guess I could do something with it to make it wearable."

"No. I can't wear it. It's green. My team has red caps, with a big *D* for Demi's on the front."

"Mmmmm."

Christopher and his mother sat at the kitchen table for a while, and then she grabbed the lucky cap again.

"I have an idea, Chris. Please get me a pair of scissors."

"What are you going to do?"

Mom's second and third fingers made a scissoring motion, and she answered,

"I'm going to cut this up into three big lucky pieces and sew one into the lining of your new cap."

"Will it work?"

"It's worth a try."

Christopher nodded.

The very next Sunday morning, Christopher pulled his bright white knee-length pants from the clean laundry basket. They smelled fresh and felt soft. He slipped on his sparkling red Demi's Bakery number 12 shirt. He put on his red cap with the secret green lining.

That *may* be why he hit a triple that day. Christopher certainly thinks so.

There's no way of knowing what will happen next spring, but one thing's for certain: Christopher's got two more pieces of lucky cap waiting in a shoe box in the back of his closet.

4

FALL

The Argument

". . . eight."

"And a half."

His mother was weakening. Christopher saw it. He could win this argument. All he needed was one more thing—the right thing—to say.

He'd already made it clear that he knew the way—backward and forward, eyes closed. He'd told her at least once that it was just a short walk—maybe five blocks. He'd said that he was practically nine; he wasn't the baby of the family anymore. The baby . . . the baby . . . yeah, that was it.

"Besides, Mom, it's beginning to get

cold. It isn't fair to Matthew to have to put all those clothes and all those blankets on him just so you can pick me up and walk me home from my piano lesson."

"Well, Matthew does hate getting all bundled up, but it's getting dark by four-thirty when your lesson is over. And I never let Greg walk home alone in the dark when he was eight."

"I'm eight and a half. And I'm a lot more careful than Greg."

"All right, Christopher. We'll try it tomorrow. You know the rules. You know the way. And Christopher, if you change your mind and want me to come and meet you, just tell Ms. Williams to call, and I'll be there in a jiff. It's only a half dozen blocks."

"That's just what I've been saying,

Mom. It's a short walk. Nothing to worry about."

"Okay. Settled. Dinner in a half hour, Chris."

Christopher hoped his mother would announce during dinner that he would be walking home alone from Ms. Williams's studio tomorrow. But Daddy had lots to tell them about his plans for their trip to the pumpkin farm on the weekend. And Greg had lots to say about the fifth-grade Horror Halloween party. And Matthew was fussy. So nothing was said.

"Ready for your piano lesson tomorrow?" his father asked when he was tucking Christopher in.

"Uh-huh. I've got that baseball song memorized."

It was the third song in the beginners' piano book. It had only five notes, but you had to use two hands to play it. There were words to the simple tune that made it a lot easier to learn and much more fun to practice.

"You're enjoying the piano, aren't you, Chris?"

"I like it. And I like Ms. Williams."

Here was Christopher's chance to tell his dad that tomorrow he'd be walking home from Ms. Williams's on his own—in the almost dark. But all of a sudden it seemed silly to say anything, so instead he gave his daddy an extra long, extra tight good-night hug.

"Yummm. Good night, Chris."

His father shut the light, and Christopher's room got dark—darker than he ever remembered it being before.

"Daddy? What time is it?"

"Bedtime. About eight."

"Right. Good night."

Eight. That was more than three hours later than it would be tomorrow when he was walking home from his piano lesson. It got a lot darker in those three hours—from four-thirty to nearly eight o'clock. A lot.

The Lesson

It was a regular Wednesday at school. Spelling. Reading. Arithmetic. Art. Assembly.

The assembly program was a Halloween safety talk by two police officers. It went on forever. The police wanted everyone to have a great Halloween, but children had to be aware of the dangers. Christopher had no idea there were so many safety rules to think about.

When school was over, Christopher walked to Ms. Williams's. She was in the middle of a lesson, as usual, so he went into the kitchen and helped himself to a glass of milk and some cookies. Ms. Williams had an antique cookie jar that was always filled with a variety of goodies. Christopher took a stick of licorice and a chocolate-covered marshmallow cookie.

Right on schedule, Ms. Williams called Christopher in. He played a scale with his right hand—up and down the keys, quick and sure. He played a scale with his left hand—up and down the keys, slow and steady.

"How'd you do with that baseball song, Chris? Will you perform it for me?"

Christopher closed the book.

"By heart," he whispered.

"By heart? Oh my!" Ms. Williams answered.

He played it once. Then a second time. Ms. Williams sang the words as he played it the second time. Once more, and this time Ms. Williams clapped her hands and tapped her feet.

"You've got me dancing, Chris."

Christopher grinned at the keyboard and then at Ms. Williams.

"Good work!" Ms. Williams said.

They opened the book and started another song. Three new notes to learn.

"It's nearly four-thirty, Chris. I can hear my next student in the kitchen. I think she's been to that cookie jar four times already. On your way, dear. And do a little extra work on that left-hand scale, okay?"

"I will. See you next week."

Christopher threw his jacket on.

"You ought to snap that shut, Christopher. The wind's picking up. Do you hear the branches hitting against my window?"

"Bye, Ms. Williams."

The Walk Home

Christopher started on the usual route home. It was getting cold, and it was getting dark. The wind skittered the dead brown leaves along the ground. Christopher tried to catch up with them, stomping down with heavy steps. He felt them crinkle under his feet.

Christopher saw the park across the street. He could take the shortcut through the ball field. It would save him a block. Why not?

The baseball diamond was empty. Christopher walked around it. He stopped between second base and third, reached down and pantomined a throw to first. Someday, he just might be a baseball star, but right now all he wanted was to get home. It was late.

The ball field was surrounded by trees—ancient ones, tall and thick, and close together. In summer, after a game, the trees made a cool, shady spot for drinking lemonade and celebrating a victory. But tonight, with just a few leaves left on the branches, and the wind blowing wildly, the trees seemed to block Christopher's way. But he had to walk through them; otherwise, this would be no shortcut.

The street lamp behind the park lit a thin path through the trees, and Christopher stepped carefully. Twigs snapped underfoot, and Christopher turned to see if there was someone behind him. There was no one. He was all alone.

Christopher put one foot in front of the other and walked toward the light. At last, he emerged from the trees.

Now where was the hole in the fence? Where? Finally, he saw it, marked by what was left of an old sweatshirt, caught on the fence wire, waving in the breeze.

It was raining now—steady, cold, noisy drops. Christopher pulled up his collar and started to walk faster. He wished for wings that would open up and let the wind lift him and carry him home. But the next gust brought only a coldness that blew through his jacket. He pulled it closed. Snap. Snap. Snap. He slid his hands into his pockets. The lining had turned to ice.

Christopher ran. Two blocks to go. The leaves on the ground no longer snapped when he stepped on them. Instead they clung to the bottom of his sneakers and made them slippery. He kept his eyes on the sidewalk.

He didn't look up until he got to the corner, to the Weavers' house. It was all decorated for Halloween—with spiderwebs strung along the trees and a skeleton swinging from the telephone pole. Jack-o'-lanterns with flickering candles stared out the windows.

The porch light went on suddenly. Christopher turned to run, but before he could move, the front door opened and a man stepped out into the rain.

"Is that you, Christopher? What are you doing out alone on a night like this?"

It was Robyn Weaver's dad, just trying to help. But the way he stood under that light, and the sound of his voice caught inside the wind, frightened Christopher. He couldn't answer.

Christopher reached the curb and stepped down. A loud horn shouted at him. He jumped back and watched the car ride past him down the street. He watched until its red lights disappeared around a corner.

Breathless, but careful this time, he crossed the street. Ahead he saw a blurry yellow light. His light. He remembered how it kept the bugs away in the summer.

He was nearly home. Twelve steps— he counted them every day. His legs were exhausted; his arms, heavy; his fingers, numb. He walked slowly. Ten. Eleven. Twelve. He leaned on the doorbell. His mother opened the door and smiled. Christopher stepped inside and pushed the door closed behind him.

Snap. Snap. Snap.